T0365822

Sparino De Birdarack

by
Barbara Williamson

Illustrated by

Alfred Yeager and
Barbara Williamson

To order additional copies of this book, contact:
Xlibris
844-714-8691
www.Xlibris.com
Orders@Xlibris.com

ISBN: 978-1-4363-4276-6 (sc)
ISBN: 978-1-4771-8122-5 (e)

Print information available on the last page

Rev. date: 03/22/2025

This book is dedicated to my daughter Kelly, my closest friend, and my granddaughters, Danielle and Kimberly, my sweet angels.

Hello, my name is

Sparino De Birdarack.

Early one summer morning, as the birds gathered by the little pond near the pine tree in the park, Sparino, a rather not so nice looking bird, was having a bird-to-bird talk with his friend. Sparino's friend is a large, beautiful parrot named Moe Zambeek.

During their talk, Sparino tells his bird buddy that he would like to write beautiful poems and love songs, and to someday share them with someone special.

Each day while working in a lumber mill as a feather-sander, he would sand birdhouses, and think of wonderful poetry. He would sand and rhyme, and rhyme and sand, and sand and rhyme some more.

He would have lunch with Moe and recite his latest poem. "Well, buddy, what do you think?" he would ask.

Moe would roll his eyes and say, "You're wasting your talents on me, Sparino, old friend; you should be on stage."

Sparino would lower his head, embarrassed, because he knew he was not very nice looking. He wished he were big and handsome like his parrot friend. He was very grateful for his friendship with Moe Zambeek.

Sparino's friend Moe worked in a different wing of the building then his friend. Moe was a feather-duster. After the wood was cut, graded, and sanded, Moe then dusted it. This very special wood is prepared for the finest birdhouses in Oregon.

Best Friends.
Best Friends.

In Moe's department, he mentioned to some of his work flock that he had a talented friend with a gift for speaking. He then mentioned it to the "king of the roost," Moe's boss, Mr. Jay Bird.

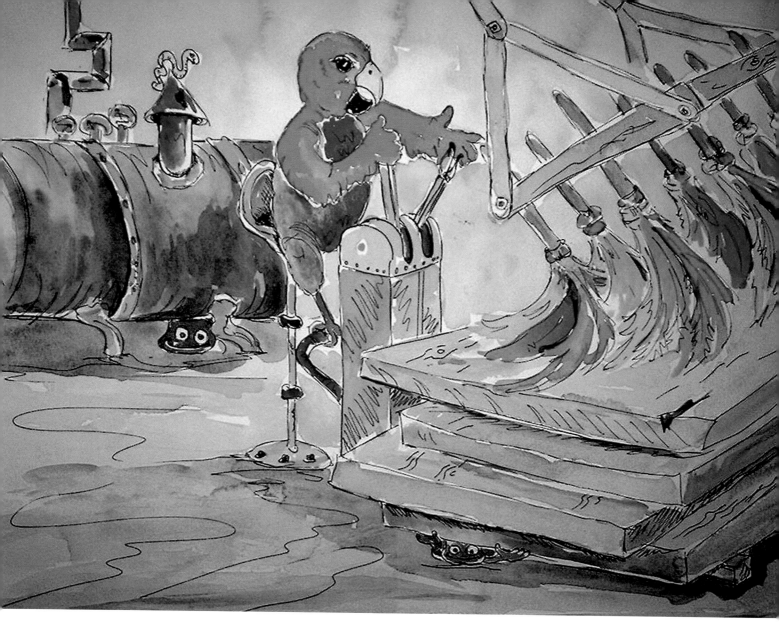

Mr. Bird was very interested because he had an opening at his radio station during the morning talk show time. The rooster roster was low because of snowbirds leaving the company. He wondered if Sparino would be available for a chirp.

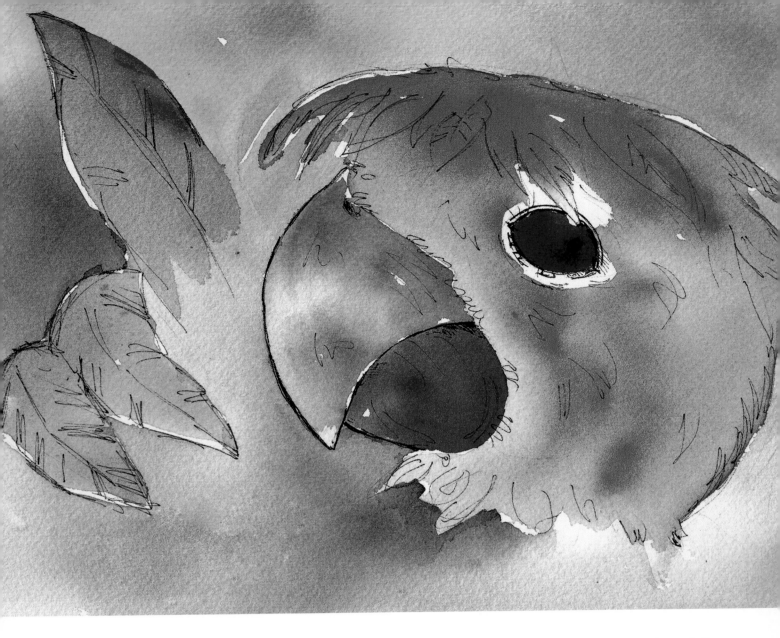

That night, Moe flew down to Sparino's house and told him the good news. Sparino was so excited, but again, he was worried about his appearance. He reminded his friend that he was not a very nice looking bird. He was happily surprised at Moe's reply, "My dear friend, I would gladly trade the way I look for the way you think."

Moe perched himself up near his friend, looked him in the eye, and said, "Sparino, we have each been given special gifts from our Creator and we need to share those gifts with our families and friends. I can not imagine never hearing all the wonderful things you've shared with me in your poetry."

Proudly, Sparino marched into Jay Bird's office on Monday and introduces himself. He recites some of his poetry and the next thing he knows he has landed the morning spot on the SQUAWK TALK radio show.

Time flew by. The rest of the week Sparino worked his feathers to the bone writing new material for the show. He was to start the new show the following Monday.

He began the first program by saying:
"Hello, my name is Sparino.
I am not a very pretty bird you know.
I guess that's why I am on the radio."

Sparino won the hearts of all the mill workers. Especially one in particular, a cute little chick that works in the west-wing fountain called THE BEST NEST YET. She had seen Sparino De Birdarack and Moe Zambeek having lunch together. She had never met them, but she had a feeling that Moe was the man on the radio.

Kelly whispered to her friend, Mag Pie, that she was much too shy to meet Sparino the famous radio poet.

She said she would rather meet his little friend. She had more in common with the little black scruffy bird, since they both seemed to be shy. She could not imagine someone like a radio personality paying attention to her. Therefore, she would settle for someone not so handsome and not so smart.

Mag Pie told Kelly she that she needed to be happy being herself. She had just as much to offer in life as anyone else. Mag told her to strive for the best, always.

Every morning Kelly listened to the radio with a smile on her face, thinking and wishing that the radio announcer was cooing those poems to her.

Time flew by. Sparino was really enjoying his new job; he was testing his wings. One morning Sparino went to the station and discovered a note from Kelly Winger. It said:

"Sparino, I'd like to meet the friend you know. I am near you everyday at lunch and sometimes I watch you munch. Please, join my friend and me, and I will treat you to some seed cake. Let's meet at the best nest yet. I'll take care of the rest," K.W.

Sparino finished his morning show and went to see his buddy, Moe. Sparino showed him the note and waited to see what Moe would say. Sparino told Moe that he was happy for him and Sparino wanted to see the person that liked his friend. A puzzled Moe said, "Fine."

Secretly, Sparino was a little sad that Kelly wanted to meet Moe; he wished she wanted to meet him.

The next day Sparino and Moe went to the fountain. They had lunch, then water; soon a seed cake was delivered to their table and over walked Kelly and Mag. They sat down and, in the introduction, Moe realizes that Kelly thinks that he is Sparino. Moe then chirped:

"Roses are red violets are blue. Moreover, I cannot rhyme worth pooh. Please, allow me to introduce my best friend, Sparino De Birdarack."

A confused Kelly sheepishly bowed her head. "You're the radio announcer aren't you?" she asked.

"I wish I was, but it's my friend Sparino here, who's the radio announcer," Moe replies.

Mag chirps up, "Then it's your friend that Kelly wants to meet."

Sparino was so amazed. He and Kelly started talking and it was love from the start.

His dream came true, now he was writing poems and love
songs for someone special. Time flew by.
Then one morning Sparino opened his show by saying:
"Hello, my name is Sparino.
I have spent a lot of time alone you know.

Now I want my dream to come true.

And it will if, Kelly, you will let me marry you."

When Sparino and Moe had lunch at the fountain, on his

plate along with a seed cake was a note reading:

"Roses are red, violets are blue.

My wonderful Sparino, I would love to marry you," K.W.

The End

Printed in the United States
by Baker & Taylor Publisher Services